STEEL FOR HIRE

GALACTIC MERCENARIES

BOOK 1

OTHER BOOKS

Dragon Riders of Osnen

Trial by Sorcery
A Bond of Flame
The Warrior's Call
The Coin of Souls
Wing of Terror
Eyes of Stone
Tooth and Claw
The Servant of Souls
Smoke and Shadow
The Dark Rider
The Song of Bones
Sword and Crown
Tides of Darkness
Wrath and Ruin

Marked by the Dragon

Scale of the Dragon
Egg of the Dragon
Call of the Dragon
Wrath of the Dragon

The Fallen King Chronicles

Dragonsphere
The Fallen King
The Valiant King
The Restored King

STEEL FOR HIRE

GALACTIC MERCENARIES

BOOK 1

RICHARD FIERCE

Dragonfire Press

e-Book ISBN: 978-1-947329-20-1

Print ISBN: 978-1-958354-24-7

First Edition: 2023

1

"WE'RE BROKE," JAYDE SAID, casting a baleful glance at Lochlan, the ship's pilot.

"We'll find another job," Gavin replied. He was always defending Loch, and Jayde hated him for it. Perhaps hate was too strong a word. She turned her fiery gaze on Gavin and frowned. Fine, she didn't *hate* him. But it really annoyed her when he stood in the way of Loch taking responsibility for his mistakes.

"You know, we wouldn't have to find another job if Loch could stick to the plan and quit screwing anything that walks on two legs."

"That's not fair, Jayde, and you know it."

Loch stood up from his chair and crossed his arms. Jayde turned to face him, and they engaged in a silent stare-down. Her green eyes bored into his blue ones. Neither one would give in, and eventually, Gavin stepped between them and smiled at Jayde.

"Come on. We both know that Loch is never going to change, so we might as well accept the fact that he's going to screw us out of a few jobs."

"Yeah, literally," Jayde muttered. "I'll be in my bunk."

She stormed off to her personal quarters, wondering for the thousandth time why she continued to put up with Loch's constant stupidity. It was like he didn't use his brain sometimes and let his second head do all the thinking. They were so close to getting a huge payday, and yet again, Loch had ruined it. The lord of a small planet had hired them to clear out a gang that had taken up residence in his city. While the rest of the crew had been doing just that, Loch had snuck away with the lord's daughter.

A servant had caught them and immediately informed her master. If it wasn't for Jayde's quick-thinking and their even quicker escape, the lord would have executed them all. As it was, Jayde wasn't sure that they had gotten away without repercussion. The rear sensors on the ship hadn't detected pursuit, but that didn't mean they were home free just yet.

Jayde entered her personal quarters and shut the door behind her. She stared at her desk, debating on whether or not she should drink a small glass of Erillian wine. It always helped calm her anger. She was fuming. Loch had managed to really screw them over on this job. Their pockets were empty and her ship needed some work, not to mention they hadn't found a high paying job in months.

She sighed and walked over to the window and stared out at the stars. The vast black landscape stretched as far as she could see. The few stars that burned on the fringe of civilization sputtered and glowed dimly.

"Even the stars are dying out here," Jayde muttered aloud.

If they couldn't find a decent gig soon, she would be forced to land on some god-forsaken outpost until she could afford to refuel the ship. When she was young and wished to see the universe, she never thought it would be in a dilapidated ship with a crew of misfits. Hell, she never thought she'd be a mercenary either, but here she was. Captain Jayde Thrin of the *Determination.*

She snorted and turned from the window just as a massive jolt rocked the ship and pitched it roughly to the side. Everything on her desk slid off the smooth polished surface and crashed to the floor. The whole vessel groaned and Jayde thought she could hear an explosion in a distant part of the ship. She staggered into the hall, stepping over fallen items on her way out. The ship jolted again and she had to throw herself bodily against a wall to keep from tumbling to the floor.

The emergency siren blared overhead, followed by Loch calling her to the bridge. If he was calling for her, then there was a serious problem. He might be a worthless womanizer, but he was a damn good pilot. Jayde hurried down the hall to the bridge, barely pausing long enough for the doors to open.

"Blast it, what's going on in here—"

The words died on her lips as she surveyed the scene. Gavin was barely standing. He was holding onto a console, struggling to keep his balance. Loch was feverishly tapping buttons on the ship's control panel and cursing vehemently. The siren continued to blare loudly, and Jayde had all she could take.

"Turn that damn thing off!"

"I'm trying," Loch shouted. "We've been hit by something and our shields are down."

"Great! They haven't finished charging yet?"

"Not quite. They're at sixty percent." Loch tapped the screen with one finger. "Sixty-five," he corrected.

"That'll have to do," Jayde said. "Turn them on."

"Aye, Captain," Loch grunted.

A few seconds later, the ship began to hum as the shields kicked on. Loch managed to straighten the ship and Jayde sat in the chair beside him and checked the rear sensors. Not far behind them, a sleek Inquisitor ship was closing the distance. Jayde ground her teeth in anger and looked at Loch.

"Nice," she muttered. "Real nice."

Loch peered at the screen and his eyes widened in surprise. "To be fair, his daughter came onto me. I hadn't even noticed her until she—"

"I don't care," Jayde interrupted. "What's done is done. But if we survive, you'll be lucky if I don't turn you in to the Convocation and collect on your bounties."

Jayde smirked as Loch immediately stopped arguing with her. His warrants with the Convocation were a sore spot. Normally, Jayde wouldn't use that weapon against him, but she was furious with him for messing up this time. They desperately needed a payday. Now they weren't just broke, they were being hunted down by the local authorities.

"We're getting a communication request," Loch said.

"Put it through," Jayde replied.

She sat up straight in her chair. Loch tapped a button on the console and the large screen that hung awkwardly above the observation deck window flickered to life and the familiar face of Lord Rasking greeted them. Jayde groaned inwardly but put on a face of bravado.

"Lord Rasking," Jayde said.

"Mercenary scum," Rasking replied. "I find it so enjoyable that I found you with your pants down, so to speak. I'll make this easy for you. Let us board you without a fight and we'll kill you and your crew quickly."

Jayde laughed in response. "Come on, Rasking. This is the crew of the *Determination*. We don't do anything easy around here. I'll tell you what. Run with your tail tucked between your legs and I won't blast your hide to dust particles immediately. I'll give you a head start."

Rasking's face scrunched into a snarl. "The only one getting blasted to pieces is going to be you." He turned to someone offscreen and ordered them to fire. The *Determination* shuddered as a barrage of laser cannon fire blasted into the side of the ship.

Jayde felt a slight tremor under her boots as the shields took the brunt of the attack. She slammed a fist onto the console, ending the video feed of Rasking's ugly smile.

"Shields down to forty-five percent!" Loch shouted.

"It's time to show this petulant lord who he's messing with," Jayde said. She pressed a button on the screen and leaned forward to speak into the microphone.

"McCready, get to the gunnery bay and return fire with the plasma turrets. I want that ship burnt to a crisp!"

Jayde hoped the old grizzled veteran wasn't asleep or passed out drunk. A few moments later, scattered bolts of light filled the sky and struck the Inquisitor ship head-on. The enemy ship's defenses glowed red under the assault.

Although the *Determination* was a cargo ship, it was equipped with the latest plasma cannons for self-defense. Jayde had learned long ago that space was, for lack of a better phrase, the wild frontier. Pirates roamed the black ocean of space, looting and pillaging anyone they came across.

"Gavin, get down there and assist McCready. If we can't get a hit on their ship, we're going to be in serious trouble."

The ship's navigator sprinted off to obey and Jayde turned her attention to the console. The shields were close to failing and their fuel was running low.

She knew they had enough to possibly get them to a recharge outpost, but it wouldn't be very far from their current position. Unless they were able to maim the Inquisitor vessel, it wouldn't be much of an escape.

A second volley of laser blasts left the *Determination* and struck Lord Rasking's ship. McCready's deep laughter came roaring through the comms speaker.

"We're about to have an opening in their defenses," the veteran said. "I'm going to light him up!"

Jayde had a sudden trepidation about possibly injuring Lord Rasking. He was a member of the Convocation, after all. The fact that he had threatened to kill her and her crew, however, gave her the boost she needed to push that fear away.

"Take it when you see it," she ordered.

"Is that the best idea?" Loch asked.

Jayde ignored him. He had some nerve asking a question like that. Why hadn't he asked himself that before gallivanting with Rasking's daughter? *Bastard,* she thought.

"Call the engine room," Jayde said.

Loch did as she requested. There was a short delay, then Klaus's voice crackled through the speaker.

"I've got some issues down here. Can I get back to you?"

There was a noise that sounded like an explosion, followed by some incoherent shouts, then the audio cut off. Jayde glanced at Loch. Her face remained impassive, but she was sure he could see the uncertainty in her eyes. She gave Loch a slight nod to let him know she had everything under control, then turned to look out the window and spotted Raking's vessel turning in an attempt to flee.

"I don't think so," she muttered. "McCready, hit that ship with everything you've got."

A rain of plasma blasts fell onto the Inquisitor ship, causing multiple explosions to erupt along the vessel. Jayde watched with grim satisfaction as Raking's ship lit up with flames. And then it exploded, sending debris flying in every direction. A shower of metal shrapnel struck the Determination's shield and bounced off, floating lazily through space.

The sudden realization that they had just killed a member of the Convocation made Jayde's stomach drop. Loch wouldn't be the only one with warrants now.

"Get us out of here," she ordered Loch. "Now."

"On it," he answered.

Jayde left the chair and headed for the lift. She needed to see what the commotion was in the engine room. It was a welcome distraction from the fear.

"What was I thinking?" she berated herself. "Now Rasking is dead and I'm screwed. We're all screwed."

The lift came to a stop and Jayde could smell smoke. She hurried down the hall and practically leaped down the short stairwell into the engine room. Now she didn't just smell smoke, she saw it. Black clouds were billowing off one of the engines. Klaus stood nearby, spraying foam onto the flames. The ship's mechanic managed to kill the fire, but Jayde could see the damage was done.

"What happened?" she asked.

Klaus whirled to face her. "You scared the hell out of me! Announce yourself next time, will you?"

"Will do," Jayde replied. "Sorry."

Klaus shook his head and set the fire extinguisher down. He tilted his head to either side, stretching his neck muscles.

"Something hit us hard, which caused a load of debris to land on the engine. I tried to remove it, but the weight of it all crushed the casing and broke the engine wall. We're lucky it didn't simply explode and destroy the entire ship."

"That's good news," Jayde said. "Is it fixable?"

"Not with what we've got onboard. We need to stop somewhere. The other engine wasn't damaged, but it's not going to be able to power the entire ship."

"Great. Let me know if anything changes down here."

Klaus grunted in reply and Jayde went back to the lift. Their already bad situation had just gotten worse.

2

THE *DETERMINATION* SHUDDERED AND groaned as it came to a stop.

Jayde's eyes snapped open and she sat up. Her dreams had been troubled and she'd spent more time lying awake than she had actually sleeping. Jayde had spent so much time traveling the universe that she always found the feeling of being on a ship that wasn't moving so odd. She hoped that would never change.

"Where are we?" she muttered to herself. Her throat was dry and her voice sounded raspy. *Ugh,* she thought. *I need something to drink.*

A quick walk from her quarters took her to the galley where she drank some water, then she headed to the observation deck to find out where Loch had landed. The pilot was still sitting at the ship's console when she arrived.

"Where are we?" she asked.

"A little place called M44. It was the only outpost we could reach with what little fuel we had. It's a nice place, from what I remember."

"Wait. You've been here before?"

"Yep. It's been a couple of years, but it still looks the same to me."

"What does the M stand for?" Jayde inquired.

"Mine. The planet itself is a giant mining operation. The outpost grew out of necessity for supplies and whatnot long before we were ever born."

"We're not going to run into any problems with some random woman's father or husband trying to kill you, are we? That would make me turn you in to the Convocation. And considering we desperately need the money, I'm tempted to do it anyway."

"Why don't you?" Loch asked.

Jayde wasn't sure if was asking the question in a serious manner or not, but she decided to give him an honest answer.

"You're the best pilot I've ever encountered outside the Convocation's military. Given our profession, I need you. It's not easy for me to admit that."

Loch's eyebrows rose in surprise and he placed his hand over his heart, exaggerating his disbelief.

"Was that a compliment?"

"Maybe," she answered. She had to turn away to keep him from seeing the smile tugging at her lips. "Don't press your luck, though." She cleared her throat and turned back to face him. "We need a new engine and fuel, and we don't have money for either. When I said we were broke, I wasn't kidding. I'm not sure what to do here. Do you have any old contacts here that would let us borrow some funds?"

"No, but I might have something better. How much do you love me?" Loch asked.

"I don't," Jayde said bluntly.

Loch reached down the front of his shirt and withdrew a silver pendant with one of the largest diamonds Jayde had ever seen.

"We can sell this," he said proudly.

"Where did you get that? That diamond has got to be at least six carats!"

"Eight, actually. I lifted it from Rasking's daughter while we were, uh …"

"Stop. I don't need or want to know. You stole jewelry from a Convocation lord's daughter?"

"I did," Loch replied. "To be fair, though, you *killed* a Convocation lord, so—"

"Don't remind me," Jayde interrupted. "Fine, just … fine. Do you think you can sell it here? This seems like a small outpost. Aren't these people poor?"

"I told you, the planet is a mine. It's a gold mine. And I don't mean that figuratively."

"That's good. See if you can get enough to buy an engine and refuel the ship. Otherwise, we're going to need to find something else to sell."

"I'll do my best," Loch said, cracking a grin at her.

"You better," Jayde threatened.

"Yeah, yeah. The docking crew just connected to our ship, so we can get some fresh air." Loch stood up and stretched. "You coming?"

"I'm going to see if we can find any work here. Something small so we can get some food back in the galley. Let's meet back here in an hour. Is that enough time for you to find a buyer for that thing?"

"Should be. If not, I'll meet you back here regardless."

"Good. See you in an hour."

Jayde left the deck and went to find McCready. She might need his muscles and intimidation in this place. She had only been to one mining outpost before, and it was full of lascivious men who hadn't seen a decent looking woman in years. McCready had gotten into a brawl that day and knocked out ten men before they gave up the chase.

She could handle herself in a fair fight, no doubt, but she wasn't prepared to enter a situation like that again. As a mercenary, she could drink, curse, and fight like the best of them, but at the end of the day, she was a woman who wanted womanly things. Things the *Determination* didn't have.

Like a bathtub. She desperately wanted a hot bath, but she didn't trust strangers to keep away from her things. Especially not on some backwater planet like this mining outpost. With McCready keeping watch, she knew there wouldn't be any issues. She reached the door to his quarters and knocked loudly. He didn't answer, but she opened the door anyway.

McCready stepped out of his washroom shirtless. A plethora of scars ran across his hairy chest, all of them carrying a story. He wasn't one to divulge the details of his past, but Jayde knew it had something to do with his service in the Convocation military. And whatever had happened must have been bad. Anytime she asked about his service, he would simply go quiet and remain that way for hours.

"I'm going down to the outpost. Will you come with me? I've got a few things to do and I could use the help."

McCready grunted. "Sure."

"Loch says he's been here before. Says it's a good place, from what he remembers."

"Where hasn't Loch been?"

The burly man seemed to be in one of his brooding moods, so Jayde figured she'd keep the small talk to a minimum.

"We need to find a gig here. Nothing major, just something to get a little food on this ship before we head back out into space."

"Food sounds good. So does a beer."

"Sure, we can get whatever you want."

The two of them made their way to the loading bay doors. The docking crew had raised a platform to the bay, which made getting down to the ground a lot easier than normal. Jayde had almost slipped down a few worn stairways at a number of other ports, so this place had just become her favorite.

She wasn't sure what to expect out of a mining outpost, but as the platform lowered them to the ground, she was pleasantly surprised. The outpost was a bustle of movement. People were shopping and selling everything from exotic foods to alien slaves. It was a wonder the Convocation put up with slavery, but Jayde had long suspended they were getting a piece of the pie. Ever since humanity had spread across the stars, they had dominated other planets and forced alien life forms to bend to their will.

That was just one of the reasons why Jayde was glad she hadn't been born on Earth. She pushed away the memories that threatened to break free of her mental cage and led McCready to a building that appeared to be a bar. She pushed the door open and blinked her eyes as the stench of rancid alcohol and sweaty bodies assailed her nostrils.

"Just once I'd like to find a bar that doesn't smell like a Turillian took a dump on the floor and then died right after," Jayde complained in a low voice.

McCready didn't say anything. He left her side and went to the bar to take a seat. Jayde was hoping to find a bath here, but given the patronage, she didn't think they even knew what a bar of soap was. She took the stool beside the veteran soldier and listened to the chorus of voices that rose in conversation around them.

It was mostly people complaining about their jobs or asking for gossip about the locals. Nothing interesting, and nothing that hinted at a quick job. Jayde was about to ask McCready to help her find a better place to drink at when one of the conversations at a nearby table caught her attention.

"The blasted things are eating my fortune away. Literally!"

Jayde offered a side-eyed glance, looking just long enough to see who was talking. It was an older man. He was gray-haired, with olive colored skin and a regal bearing about him. Jayde could tell money when she saw it. And this man had deep pockets, she was sure of that. The material of his clothing was worth a decent chunk of change alone.

"What about the Convocation? Didn't you say they were sending help?"

"Yeah, but it's going to be almost a week before they get here. Those aliens will have eaten everything in my mines by then! I'd hire some of the folks here, but they're afraid to go underground. There are whispers that the mines are haunted or some such nonsense. My mines aren't haunted with anything but those blasted lyscrens."

The more he talked, the more it sounded like something Jayde and her crew could handle. Lyscrens were a small, dog-sized alien that fed on precious minerals. They were usually found on mining planets for obvious reasons. The small creatures were regarded as harmless pests more than anything, and they were easy to kill, too.

Jayde nudged McCready with her elbow. "You hearing this?"

She turned to see him gulping down a tall glass of amber colored liquid. He offered a deep burp when he finished and looked past her to the table where the old man sat, then looked at her and shrugged.

"You know where I stand," he said. "As long as we get paid, I'll kill anything."

That was true. Jayde had hired McCready for several reasons, but the main reason being that he wasn't afraid to get his hands bloody. None of the members of her crew were, really. But McCready was a beast, a king among men when it came to battle. Jayde smiled at the soldier and listened to the old man continue talking about his gold mine.

The barkeep asked her what she'd like to drink and she asked for water. He smirked and poured her a glass of orange tinted liquid.

"What's that?" she asked.

"Water," the barkeep replied. "The pipes don't hold up very well around here. The clay gets into the pipes and gives the water some color. No one's ever died from drinking it, so I continue to serve it."

"Why don't you get the pipes fixed?" Jayde asked.

"I have. Three times in the last year. It's cheaper to leave them alone. No one comes in here looking for water, anyway."

"What do you know about the gentleman sitting at the table there?" Jayde motioned with a nod of her head, trying to keep from looking conspicuous.

"That's Luther. He owns one of the mines a few miles from here. He's got an infestation of lyscrens, from what I hear. Bad for business, those things. The mine has been in his family for generations, but if he doesn't deal with those aliens, he'll be learning really quick what being poor feels like."

"Good to know." She sniffed the water in the glass. It had no smell, but she didn't feel comfortable drinking orange water. She slid the glass away from her and McCready snatched it up and downed it.

Jayde gave him a disgusted look and stood up. She ran her hands down the front of her shirt, smoothing out the material, then she walked over to Luther's table. The old man stopped talking and looked up at her curiously.

"Can I help you, girl?" he asked.

"No, but I can help you. I'm Jayde, and I'm going to clear those pests out of your mines."

Judging by the hopeful look in Luther's eyes, Jayde knew she'd just found their next employer.

3

"GEAR UP," JAYDE SAID to Lochlan as he stepped into the ship.

She had been waiting for him to get back so they could meet Luther and catch a ride with him to the mines. She and the other two, McCready and Gavin, had changed into their battle armor already. It resembled wet suits used for diving in that it was thin and versatile, but it was strong enough to take a direct hit from a laser.

"For what?" Loch asked.

"I found us a quick gig to make some cash. We're going into one of the mines to clear out some lyscrens. It shouldn't take more than a few hours."

"You're good," Loch said with a hint of surprise. "But I'm better. I sold the pendant for a nice price."

"How much?" Jayde asked.

"Enough to get a new engine. It's being delivered within the next thirty minutes."

Jayde suppressed a grin. "That's why I keep you around," she said. "Sometimes you make yourself useful. Go get changed. Those lyscrens might be harmless, but you never know what else might be down there. Tell Klaus to get the engine bay ready for the replacement, will you?"

Loch mock saluted and disappeared down the hallway. Jayde rubbed the back of her neck and sighed quietly. Her lack of sleep was catching up to her, but she didn't have time to be tired. The quicker they finished this job, the quicker they could get off this rock and find a job that paid enough to let them retire. That was the dream, anyway.

She stepped out of the ship and onto the platform where McCready and Gavin were waiting. The old soldier was looking over his gun. It was a Silver Flux rifle, standard issue for soldiers in the Convocation military. The gun was capable of letting off seven hundred laser rounds per minute. Jayde didn't know much about the military, but she knew about fighting and weapons. And McCready's gun was a beautiful weapon. It was modeled after a bullpup rifle design on Earth, but much more powerful.

"Do you think it's a good idea to bring that into the mines?" she asked the veteran. "I don't know about you, but I don't want to go deaf when you start shooting it."

"I don't plan on using it unless things go south," McCready answered. "Since Luther said he had some flamethrowers we could use, I'll use one of those. That's a much better option for dealing with lyscrens in a confined space. You can kill more with less effort." He grinned.

"It's been a while since I've seen one. A lyscren, I mean. I brought my pistol," she said, patting her side, "but only as a last resort. I'm with you, I'd much rather burn them to a crisp."

Gavin was wearing the same type of armor as Jayde, but he didn't have a weapon. While he was able to hold his own in a fight, he was more of a pacifist. The only reason he'd joined Jayde's ragtag mercenary band was because she had saved his life during a battle between two Convocation lords in a land dispute. She guessed he must have felt obligated to follow her, but she had never forced him to join her.

They were each just normal people looking for a place to belong in the universe, a place to feel safe. A place to find rest from the struggle to survive in a universe determined to chew people up and spit them out.

"Sorry," Loch said as he strode out onto the platform. "Klaus needed a hand moving the damaged engine. The crane he was using got stuck and needed a little push."

"You all set?" Jayde asked.

"Yeah. Let's roast some alien hide, shall we?"

They all walked down the platform to the ground and headed for the edge of town. Luther was waiting for them in a solar-powered transport vehicle. He waved them over with a smile. Jayde was familiar with his type. They always threw money at their problems and expected them to go away. While that was normally the case for people like Luther, Jayde knew too that some problems couldn't be solved with money.

"Those are some nice uniforms," Luther said. "Are they laser resistant?"

"They are," Jayde answered.

Luther whistled. "They must have cost a pretty penny."

"They weren't cheap, no. But they have proven their worth time and again."

Jayde got into the vehicle, choosing to sit in the front with Luther. The other three climbed into the rear portion which was designed for hauling freight. Luther shifted the vehicle into drive and they began moving along the worn dirt road. Jayde always found it fascinating how some places were so similar even though they were thousands of miles away from each other.

"Have you been into the mines since the lyscrens took up residence?" Jayde asked.

"Just once. It was a few days ago when one of the miners said he saw something out of the ordinary. I went down to investigate, but I didn't see anything."

"You didn't see any lyscrens?"

"Oh, I saw those all right. They're everywhere down there. No, I meant the thing the miner saw. He said it looked like a man, but whatever it was acted strangely. I didn't see it or anything like it, so I figured he must have been seeing things."

The way Luther's tone changed as he talked told Jayde that he knew more than what he was revealing. She kept that in the back of her mind in case they ran into trouble in the mines. If there was one thing Jayde hated more than anything, it was being surprised.

"When we finish the job, where should we meet you? Will you be staying nearby?"

Luther nodded. "Yeah, I'll hang around for a while. If you aren't done within three or four hours, I'll head back to town. I don't want to make you walk back, so you can keep this in case I'm not back when you're finished."

He handed her a communication device that reminded Jayde of a cellular phone. She'd never owned one, but she'd seen pictures in a book once. It was the way people on Earth communicated with one another before technology advanced.

"So, what brings you to M44?" Luther asked. "We don't see a lot of visitors here."

"One of the engines in my ship was damaged. This was the closest place."

"Well, it turned out to be for the best. For me, anyway. I'm afraid if I had to wait until the Convocation showed up, those blasted aliens would have eaten all my gold."

"I'm glad we can help," Jayde replied. "Just out of curiosity, why didn't any of your miners want to make some extra money by killing the lyscrens?"

Luther shifted uncomfortably in his seat and kept his gaze locked forward. "The thing one of them saw … well, they think the mines are haunted. They won't go back in there until they're convinced that it's safe. It's nonsense if you ask me."

"Perception is reality," Jayde said. It was something her mother used to tell her.

"That's true," Luther agreed. "That's very true."

They spent the rest of the ride in silence. The mines were two miles north of the outpost. The area was a vast desert and by the time they reached the mine, Jayde could feel sweat rolling her down back. She grimaced in disgust. The vehicle slowed and stopped as Luther engaged the brakes.

"This is the main entrance," he said, pointing toward the cavernous opening in the sand. "It goes down a few hundred feet before flattening out, then it's mostly level. There are three floors, but as far as I'm aware, the lyscrens are only on the top two. My family's been mining here for a few generations, so it's basically a maze down there."

Jayde got out of the vehicle and looked around. There was nothing but desert sand as far as she could see in any direction.

"Let's get to it," she said. She followed Luther to a small shack that stood beside the mine entrance.

"This is where we keep some of the tools," he said. "There's a couple of flamethrowers in here that we use to melt the rock when it's too strong to dig through. They should be fully fueled up." Jayde stood outside the shack and waited while Luther checked them over. He handed one to her, which she promptly passed to the others until all four of them had one.

"These are military grade," Luther said. He used Jayde's flamethrower to explain how they worked. "They're liquid-operated, so that small tank on the side there pressurizes the gas in order to push it through the tubes. It feeds up through these tubes. This tube leads to the fuel tanks, which creates the pressure that expels the liquid. This other tube leads to the ignition chamber where it all mixes together. This flame here at the end will ignite the fuel when you pull the trigger."

"Seems simple enough," McCready said. He strapped the tank portion onto his back and activated the ignition flame. The veteran turned away from everyone and pulled the trigger. A strong line of flames roared from the end of the barrel and a wave of heat washed over everyone.

"They can be fun to play with," Luther said, "But be aware of the fact that the flames deoxygenate the surrounding air. Without air, you die. The mask on the side is connected to an oxygen tank, so make sure you're wearing it before you burn anything."

"Thanks for the warning," Jayde said. "Anything else we should know?"

Luther drew nearer to her and lowered his voice. "If you see anything odd down there, let me know when you come back up."

Jayde looked him in the eyes, wondering if he'd elaborate on what he meant. The old man just smiled and turned towards the others.

"Thank you all for helping save my livelihood. You'll be well compensated."

Now that her curiosity was piqued, she wanted to know what the miners were so afraid of. Was there some other type of alien down there? There were numerous alien races that resembled humans and walked upright, but none that she could think of that would live as a recluse in a dark mineshaft. Well, if they found anything other than lyscrens down there, whatever it was better hope Jayde and her crew didn't accidentally burn it.

"I'll take the lead," McCready said, then he disappeared into the mine's dark entrance. Loch went next, then Jayde followed and Gavin brought up the rear.

The blackness was absolute. Jayde paused in the darkness and waited for her eyes to adjust to the gloom. The flamethrower's ignition source lit up the area a few steps ahead, but otherwise, it offered almost no help for her vision.

"See anything yet?" Jayde asked.

"Nothing," McCready said from up ahead. "The ground slopes down just like he said, so I doubt we'll encounter anything until we reach the actual mining area."

They began the descent down into the inner depths of the mineshaft. The only sounds were the rustling of their armor and their breathing. As they continued lower, Jayde noticed a difference in the temperature. It was getting cooler. She was thankful for that. The heat above had started to give her a headache.

After what seemed like an eternity, they reached level ground. The shaft ahead was illuminated by faint glowing stones that were spaced every eight feet. The stones were the size of a man's fist and emitted a dull blue light.

"Pretty," Gavin said from behind her. Jayde thought so, too.

"I see movement," McCready said. They moved forward as a group, each person keeping their eyes peeled for lyscrens. As they reached the end of the tunnel, it split in two directions. One went left and the other continued straight. There was nothing there.

"Weird," the old soldier muttered. "I swore I saw shadows. Maybe it was the light—"

A scream from behind Jayde made her heart leap inside her chest. She turned around to see the glowing eyes of a lyscren.

4

THE LYSCREN HAD MOTTLED green and yellow skin that resembled the scales of a snake. Its eyes were large—with dilated pupils—and seemed to hold a madness in them. The creature's mouth was clamped onto Gavin's exposed right hand. Foam dripped from its jowls and blood was flowing freely from the wound. Jayde reached for her pistol, but a wave of heat erupted from behind her.

She staggered backward and to the left, throwing herself bodily against the cool wall of the mine. Loch stepped past her, his flamethrower sending a concentrated blast of flames at the lyscren.

The creature yelped like a dog and let go of Gavin, then quickly fled past them, escaping into the tunnel. Everyone stood still for a moment, either shocked or confused at what had just happened.

"Did that thing bite you?" McCready asked Gavin.

"It sure did," Gavin replied, holding his hand at the wrist. "It burns like hellfire, too."

Jayde stepped closer and knelt in front of him. "Let me see it."

Gavin held his hand up for inspection. His fingers were trembling. Jayde eyed the wound intently. It wasn't very deep, but it was ugly. The skin of his palm had been torn straight down the center. Blood pooled into his palm, ending her scrutiny.

"Does anyone have some cloth? It's not deep, but it needs to be covered."

She looked at McCready and Loch, but they both shrugged. Jayde couldn't be mad at them. Lyscrens were supposed to be harmless, so why would they need medical supplies for a quick gig like this? Jayde stood up and looked Gavin in the eyes.

"Are you all right?"

Gavin swallowed hard and nodded. "I-I'm fine. It just surprised me. One second, I was walking behind you, then the next thing I knew a pain shot through my hand. The girl scream was involuntary, trust me."

Loch snickered but Jayde ignored him. She didn't think Gavin's wound was anything to be concerned about, but it was puzzling that the lyscren had attacked him in the first place.

"Do you need to go back up and let Luther bandage it up for you?" Jayde asked.

"No, I'm good," Gavin replied. "I'll just use my shirt. Like I said, it just surprised me. Other than a little burning, it's fine now."

"You're sure?"

"Positive," Gavin said. He pulled his shirt off and wrapped it around his hand, then tied it around his wrist. "Let's fry these little bastards and get back to the ship."

"You're speaking my language," McCready grunted.

Jayde stared at Gavin a moment more. If he said he was good, then she had to believe him. McCready turned and led them down the tunnel that the lyscren had run down. It was straight and level, but it wasn't as illuminated as the one they just left.

"Keep your guard up," the soldier said. "After that little surprise, there's no telling what else we'll see down here."

Jayde thought about what Luther had told her. The miner who had seen something so scary, he believed the mine to be haunted and wouldn't come back to work. On a planet like this, there weren't many options available to earn a living. Whatever the man had seen, it certainly had shaken him enough to give up his livelihood.

"Movement to the left. Masks up," McCready warned.

A large pack of lyscrens was crowded around a vein of gold that glittered along the wall. Jayde slipped her oxygen mask over her face just in time to see a streak of fire light up the tunnel as it washed over the aliens. Screeches and yelps echoed in the chamber as the liquid fire stuck to the lyscren's scaly skin and burned them.

One of the creatures tried to run, but Loch kicked it in the face as it tried to maneuver around him. The blow snapped its neck and it collapsed in the dirt. The sight of its melting flesh made Jayde want to gag.

The other aliens collapsed as well, their death cries weakening as the flames devoured their bodies. Once the lyscrens stopped moving, Jayde walked over to where they had been eating the gold.

"How do these things eat gold, anyway?" she asked.

McCready came over and pointed the end of his flamethrower at the vein. "See how the gold is dripping down right here?"

Jayde peered closely and saw the gold wasn't solid as she expected, but was wet and slowly dripping down the wall. She looked up at the soldier curiously.

"These little beasts have glands in their tongues that produce chemicals that react to metal, dissolving it. When they lick something, the glands push the chemicals out through the tip of their tongue. The chemical hits the metal and starts liquifying it."

"Sounds like you know a lot about them," Jayde said. "What kind of chemical is it?"

McCready shrugged. "I don't know the name of it. We encountered lyscrens all the time in the Convocation. ET's are the first ones on an unmapped planet, and lyscrens are almost always the first thing they encounter."

"ET's?" Loch asked.

"Expansion Teams," McCready clarified. "Once an unmapped planet is identified, they are the first boots on the ground. Most unmapped planets don't have intelligent life, which is why we aren't aware of them to begin with, but you never know about animal-like aliens. The ET's go in and make sure it's safe."

Jayde looked back at the gold and saw that it had stopped dripping. She dabbed her finger in it and found it was still liquid.

"Interesting," she said. "We didn't come down here for a science lesson, though. Let's keep moving."

McCready took the lead again and led them through the maze of tunnels. They encountered small packs of lyscrens in almost every tunnel, but none of them attacked. Jayde was beginning to think that the one that bit Gavin must have something wrong with it. Dogs were able to contract rabies, so maybe there was some sort of alien disease similar to rabies that the lyscren had contracted.

"The tunnel divides up here," McCready said. "One goes left and one goes right, but it looks like they converge back together a little way down. Should we split up to cover more ground?"

Jayde didn't like the idea of splitting their group up, but it would help speed up the process if they broke off occasionally. She debated the decision a moment longer, then pointed to the tunnel on the right. "Gavin and Loch, you two take that one. McCready and I will take this one. We'll see you shortly."

The team broke apart and went down each tunnel. Jayde walked behind McCready, peering into the dark and looking for movement. When Luther said the mine was overrun, she expected to see a lot more lyscrens than what they'd encountered so far.

They followed the tunnel for a few hundred feet before they heard a noise ahead. It sounded like something was coming towards them. There were no lights, so it was pitch black around them except for the ignition flames on their flamethrowers. All Jayde could see was McCready's back. He tensed up and Jayde prepared to move beside him and unleash her fire.

"Woah," a voice echoed at them. "Don't fry me."

Jayde frowned as she peeked around McCready's large form. "Loch?"

"The one and only," he said.

She heard his boots crunching the dirt before she saw his shadowy outline. They closed the distance between each other and Jayde finally saw Loch's face as it became visible under the light of McCready's flamethrower. His face looked eerie in the dim light. Jayde looked over his shoulder into the darkness.

"Where's Gavin?"

"I don't know," Loch answered. "He was walking behind me, then he said something weird and rushed ahead of me. I thought maybe he looped around to you two. He's not here?"

"No, we haven't seen him," Jayde said. "What did he say?"

"He said 'it's starting,' whatever that means."

"That's it?" McCready asked.

"Yeah. It wasn't like he was saying it to me, either. He just sort of muttered it, then took off. I don't think I've ever seen him run that fast before."

"Great." Jayde sighed in frustration. "This was supposed to be a quick job. In and out. If we have to walk back to the outpost, I'm going to kill someone."

"Just kill the lyscrens," Loch joked. "That'll get rid of your anger."

Jayde glared at the pilot until his smirk was gone.

"We need the cash, so let's finish this job," Jayde said. "We stick together from now on. I'm sure we'll find Gavin while we're clearing the tunnels."

"That sounds good to me, but why would Gavin run off in the dark like that?" Loch seemed to be growing uneasy.

"I don't know," Jayde replied.

"It might have something to do with that bite," McCready said. "Lyscrens don't attack people. I've encountered enough of them to know. If it was sick or something, it's possible the infection got into Gavin's blood when it bit him."

Jayde didn't want to accept that theory, but she knew it was likely the answer to his sudden odd behavior.

"We can worry about that once we find him," she said. "Let's keep moving."

The three of them reached the end of the tunnel, which opened into a small circular chamber supported by steel beams. Four tunnels all intersected at the chamber. The one Loch and Gavin had gone down was to the right. The tunnel directly across from the one they had just exited was partially caved in. Jayde doubted they would be able to get through, so that left the tunnel to their left.

"He must have gone that way," McCready said.

Jayde had to agree. Aside from being too small, the dirt of the caved in tunnel didn't appear to have been disturbed at all. Again, Jayde considered what Luther had said about the mine being overrun. That didn't seem to be the case, especially as they went further into the tunnels. They also hadn't seen any of the creatures since Gavin's disappearance. Was it just a coincidence?

"What's that noise?" Loch asked.

Jayde held her breath and listened. There was a scratching sound coming from the tunnel to their left. She exchanged glances with Loch and McCready, then entered the tunnel. She held the end of her flamethrower up, prepared to scorch anything that wasn't Gavin.

The scratching sound continued intermittently, but it was growing louder as she walked. She could hear Loch and McCready behind her, but she ignored their footsteps and focused on the scratching noise. It almost sounded like something sharp was scraping on a rock. Was Gavin injured and trying to make noise so they could find him? Jayde increased her pace but kept her guard up.

If you see anything odd down there, let me know when you come back up. Luther's words echoed in her mind over and over, a haunting tune that was beginning to make her question whether coming down here was a good idea.

Ahead, Jayde could see the tunnel opened up into a larger chamber. If she wasn't mistaken, it sounded like the scratching noise was coming from there. She looked over her shoulder to make sure the other two were still following her. McCready offered a slight nod. Something wasn't right about this job. Something wasn't right about this entire place.

Fear was beginning to grow in her stomach. It churned within her, worming its way up her throat. She thought she was going to be sick, but she didn't know why. Not until she smelled it. The scent was horrible and reminded her of a very dark memory.

A few more steps.

Jayde stepped into the chamber. In the far corner, something was moving around. It was hunched down, whatever it was. Jayde paused.

"I've got this," McCready said. She looked at him just as he scrunched his face in disgust. "What's that stench?" he growled.

She didn't say anything. Instead, she slowly walked toward the moving form. As she and

McCready drew closer, their flamethrowers illuminated the area. A lyscren lay on its side in a pool of blood. Something was hunched down in front of it, ripping entrails out. The dead lyscren's claws scratched the wall every time the creature tore something from it.

"That explains the scratching," Jayde whispered.

The form in front of the lyscren stopped moving. Jayde and McCready lifted their flamethrowers, ready to incinerate the creature. It slowly stood up straight and Jayde realized that it wasn't a creature at all. It was …

"Gavin?"

As the man turned around, Jayde saw that it was Gavin. Or what used to be Gavin. When his milky white eyes met hers, the horrid memory she had kept locked away broke free of its prison and she screamed.

5

JAYDE WAS TWELVE WHEN fire rained from the sky.

The weather had been perfect all day, with no storms or clouds to hide the sunlight, so Jayde had spent the last few hours playing with her friends at the playground. They were playing a popular Erillian game where one person would draw on the ground with chalk and the others would try to guess what was being drawn without looking.

Jayde had her back turned and was looking up at the sky. She'd grown a fascination with seeing the universe. Ochillon was a great place, but she wanted to know what else was out there. She played Erillian games with her friends, but she had never actually seen an Erillian. Her father had told her they were nice aliens, but they were an exception to the rule. Most sentient alien life hated humans for a reason Jayde didn't know.

"Is it a tree?" her friend Hannah asked.

"No, it's not," Aria replied. "Keep guessing."

"A dragon?" Jayde asked.

"Nope. It does have wings, though."

Something flashed in the sky and Jayde turned to look in the direction of whatever it w`as. She couldn't see what it was, but it glinted like metal. Then a second one appeared, and then a third. Soon the sky was filled with them—flashing metal-like things that streaked down through the atmosphere toward the ground. At first, Jayde thought it was a meteor shower. As the things began crashing into the ground, people shouted warnings to each other to watch out for the falling debris.

The ground trembled beneath her feet and then one of the metal things flew overhead and slammed into a tree. There was a loud crack as the tree snapped in half and the metal object *clunked* to the ground.

"What is that thing?" Hannah asked.

"I don't know, but we should probably go home. It could be something bad."

"It doesn't look bad," Hannah replied. "It looks like a capsule I've seen at my dad's work."

Hannah walked closer and Jayde had a bad feeling creeping into her stomach. The shouting she'd heard had stopped, but she didn't know if the things had stopped falling from the sky.

"Hannah," Jayde said, "don't get too close to it. Let's just go."

"It's fine," Hannah said. "It's not even hot from falling." She reached out and touched the surface of the capsule. "See?" she said. "It's fine."

As if on cue, the top portion of the capsule opened with a hissing sound that made Jayde's heart skip a beat. It must have scared Hannah too, for she jumped back quickly.

"I'm with Jayde," Aria finally spoke. "I don't think we should be here with that thing. I'm going home."

Aria left them and Jayde stared after her for a moment. *She's the smartest one of us,* Jayde thought. When she turned back to look at Hannah, her friend had already pulled the capsule door open and was leaning inside of it.

"Hannah!" Jayde shouted. "Get out of there—"

Hannah's blood-curdling scream drowned out the last of Jayde's words. Jayde could feel her heart throbbing and thought it was going to burst out of her chest. She took a step toward Hannah to see what was wrong, but Hannah pulled away from the capsule and turned around.

Jayde screamed in horror. Hannah's face was gone. The flesh had melted and was dripping down onto her chest. Hannah's mouth was opened in a silent cry, her vocal cords obliterated. Jayde turned and fled, running toward her home as fast as her legs would move, fear and desperation pushing her beyond her physical limits.

She found her father first. He was standing in the front yard, eyes up at the sky, watching the remaining capsule fall to the ground. It reminded her of the many times she had seen him storm watching. She ran to him and wrapped her arms around his waist tightly, tears streaming down her cheeks.

"What's happening?" she asked. "What are those things? They burned Hannah's face off!"

Her father didn't offer an answer, but he offered her comfort by placing a reassuring hand on her shoulder. She sobbed quietly for a moment, but there was a peace and confidence her father exuded that calmed her and pushed the fear away.

"Let's go inside," he said.

As the first few hours passed, very little seemed out of the ordinary. Her dad had called Hannah's parents and confirmed that Hannah was seriously injured. Jayde felt terrible leaving her behind the way she did, but the doctors who were taking care of Hannah said it was probably the best thing she could have done. Whatever had been inside that capsule could have caused the same injury to her.

Jayde's parents watched the flat-screened glass device in the wall that normally provided entertainment. Tonight, however, they were watching the newscaster explain what the government believed had happened.

"They're empty capsules from an abandoned ship outside of orbit," the cheery man said to the camera. "Convocation scientists have begun opening them only to find nothing inside. Aside from the danger of being struck by them as they fell, there seems to be no reason for alarm."

"Tell that to Hannah," Jayde whispered at the screen.

As the sunlight faded and the shadow of the night grew, the horrible truth became known. People began dying in multitudes. A few here and there. Then hundreds. Then thousands. By the time morning came, millions had succumbed to a foreign virus that ravaged the immune system. Animals seemed unaffected, but the human population of Ochillon was decimated.

Those who didn't die got to see the nightmare continue to unfold. The corpses of their friends and families rose and walked, feeding on anything that had flesh and blood. The Convocation issued warnings across every network to stay indoors and to keep away from the windows. Eventually, the warnings stopped. The feed on the screen became a blank canvas and they stopped hearing anything about the world outside their home.

Jayde knew her father was sick when he started bleeding from his eyes. He shared a whispered conversation with her mother, and then he left the house and never came back. Jayde didn't know where he had gone, but as she grew older, she realized that he had left so that he wouldn't kill his own family when he turned.

She didn't use the word 'zombie' when referring to the dead people walking around the streets. It seemed too unreal, too much like something from a book or a movie. And so, Jayde and her mother began calling them sleepers.

The sleepers took over everything, forcing those who were immune to the disease to go into permanent hiding. Jayde refused to live in the shadows, refused to let these dead bodies rule unchecked. When her mother fell ill and turned, Jayde killed her by parting her head from her shoulders. It was the first of the sleepers she killed, but as the days turned to weeks, she lost count of the kills.

There were only ten people left alive that she knew of when the Convocation made one final call for the living. A single ship would land to provide a rescue, and then they would drop a nuclear bomb on the planet. Jayde was the last one to reach the ship, an army of sleepers not far behind her. As the rescue ship left Ochillon behind, Jayde remembered that it was her birthday.

It was funny how that worked out. The day her new life began was the same day her old life had started. And ended. At thirteen years old, she finally got to see the stars. Naively, she thought that the events on Ochillon had to be the worst thing that could happen to her, that things could only get better going forward.

How wrong she was.

One of the survivors was infected. He killed most of the ship's crew before anyone realized what was happening. Jayde grabbed a laser rifle, fumbling with the heavy weapon and trying to point the end at the sleeper.

"Torch him!" someone screamed.

Jayde lifted the gun and froze. She couldn't pull the trigger and she didn't know why. Down on Ochillon she had killed hundreds, maybe a thousand of them. Yet now she was immobile with fear. Sweat collected in her palms.

"Torch him!" the same voice cried.

The sleeper came toward her quickly. Though dead, the corpses could move just as fast as they had in life. When she had nightmares, the sleepers were always faster than her. Their hands always grabbed her; their teeth always ripped through her flesh. The weight of the rifle was too much and it slipped from her hands, clanging loudly on the metal floor of the ship.

And then the sleeper was in front of her, his milky white eyes gazing at her, staring into her soul. She was going to die. After all of the fighting she had done to survive, now she was going to die.

"Torch him!"

6

"TORCH HIM!"

Loch's voice broke through Jayde's reverie and she looked over at McCready. His face poured sweat and he looked like he had seen a ghost. Jayde looked back at Gavin and knew what had to be done. There was no saving him, no cure for what he had become. He came at her, snarling like a wild animal. Yet as she tried to pull the trigger, she found the same fear from when she was a child had overtaken her senses. She couldn't move.

Jayde opened her mouth to tell McCready to do it, to immolate Gavin in flames, but words failed her. Loch appeared between them then and fire roared from the barrel of his flamethrower. Intense heat and the smoke of charred flesh enveloped Jayde and she snapped out of it. She jumped backward, away from the danger and watched in horror as Gavin's melting corpse dropped to the ground.

"What the hell were you waiting on?" Loch demanded angrily, turning around to face her. "He almost killed you. Both of you!"

Jayde cleared her throat. "I'm sorry, I … I don't know what happened."

Loch's anger faded with the flames of Gavin's corpse and he looked from her to McCready, then back at her. "Are you two all right? You both look like death walked over your graves."

"I'm fine," Jayde lied to him.

McCready didn't say anything, but he wiped the sweat from his face with the crook of his arm. Jayde stared at Gavin's body in silence. How had the disease from Ochillon spread to a distant mining planet on the outskirts of civilization?

"The lyscren," she whispered softly.

"What?" Loch took a step closer to her.

"The lyscren," she repeated, meeting his concerned gaze. "The lyscren that bit him must have had it."

"Had what? What are you talking about?"

"I've seen this before," Jayde replied. "Gavin was turned into a sleeper."

"A sleeper? I'm sorry, can you explain what the hell you're talking about?"

"I've seen it, too," McCready finally spoke.

Jayde had never seen the soldier so shaken up before. He was always the strong one, the muscle of their little enterprise. To see McCready afraid of something ... it seemed unnatural.

"When I was in the military, I saw them. We called them dredges. They're dead, but not dead. They don't have any brain power, just raw instincts. You always ask about my scars," McCready said, looking at Jayde. "This is why I don't like talking about them. All but two of my squad were killed. Wren and I were the only ones who escaped. No, not escaped. Got away. You can never escape this ..." McCready waved his hand toward what remained of Gavin.

"I'm so sorry, McCready," Jayde said to the big man. "If I'd have known, I would never have brought it up."

"Don't worry about it," he said gruffly. "How could you have known? The Convocation has been tight-lipped about the dredges since they first encountered the things."

The three of them stood in silence. Jayde was having trouble wrapping her mind around the fact that Gavin was lying dead not five feet away. The tears would come, but not now. There was no time for grief. She swallowed hard and ran her dry tongue over her parched lips.

"We need to do something about the lyscren that did this to Gavin. That thing can't be allowed to run around freely. If it got into the town and started biting people, that disease would destroy this place. I've seen it first-hand. We can't leave until it's dead."

"I agree," McCready said. "You two stay here and keep watch for any of the beasts that come through here. I'm going down to the second level to force the rest of them topside. Once we're certain we've fried them all, we can get out of here."

Jayde nodded weakly in agreement. She'd suddenly lost the desire to finish the job, but they couldn't leave without getting paid. Without the money for fuel, they wouldn't be able to get off the planet.

"Be thorough, but be quick," Jayde said. "We've got to inform the locals about this. They need to be prepared in case there are more infected lyscrens running around."

McCready left without saying anything. He disappeared into the darkness and Jayde hoped that nothing ill would befall him. Everything had gone so far off the rails she couldn't believe this all wasn't a dream, a nightmare of hellish proportion.

"What did you mean when you said you've seen this before?" Loch asked, breaking the silence.

"My homeworld was destroyed by the disease that turned Gavin into a sleeper," Jayde said. "No one has ever explained where the disease came from or why it hit our planet. Ochillon's population was trending to rival Earth's before …" she paused. *No. I won't relive those memories again.* "… before the disease struck. An entire civilization was wiped out within a few days."

Loch's expression had grown somber. "You were on Ochillon? I never knew that. I've never been able to get a straight answer about what happened there. It seems no one knows the story, only that the planet was placed in quarantine. No one's been heard from since."

"That's because they're all dead. All of them. Every last person. Except me."

Jayde watched Loch's mouth open to say something, but nothing came out. He pursed his lips and stared into the darkness around them. Jayde walked over to Gavin's body and knelt beside him. The flames had died, leaving behind a charred mess. She thought back to when she'd first met him and had to blink rapidly to force the tears back.

"Is it just me, or is it really quiet down here?" Loch asked.

He was right. Jayde tilted her head and listened. It was completely silent aside from their breathing. Jayde motioned for Loch to follow her and they retreated to the chamber with the intersecting tunnels.

"We'll wait here and see what happens," she said.

It seemed like hours had passed before anything happened. Jayde noticed the crunching of dirt and lifted her flamethrower, ready to take her revenge for Gavin's death on any lyscren that showed itself.

The noise grew louder and Jayde's finger twitched on the trigger of her weapon. She steadied her breathing and counted in her mind to keep her focus. *There,* she thought. There was movement. A shadowy outline was closing in on her and Loch.

"Did you see anything?" McCready's deep voice rang out.

"Oh, thank God you said something," Jayde said. "I was about to light you up."

"Thanks for not doing that," the soldier said. "We've got a problem, though. I didn't find anything down on the second level. There was evidence that the lyscrens have been down there recently. Droppings and melted gold veins, but nothing fresh. I think the creatures have abandoned the mine, aside from the ones we've already killed."

"I don't know. Maybe there's another way out of the tunnels. The lyscren that bit Gavin went deeper into the mine. It would have passed us if it went out the way we came in, and nothing got by me."

"Me either," Loch said.

"I didn't see any other exits when I was down there, but it's possible I missed something. Either way, there was nothing down there. I say we get paid and get off this cursed rock as quick as possible."

"We can't leave Gavin down here," Jayde snapped. "Or did you forget that he died?"

McCready frowned. "What are we supposed to do with him? Look at him, Jayde. He's basically a pile of ash. If we tried to move him, he'd disintegrate in our hands."

Jayde knew that was true, but she felt like he needed to be put to rest somewhere better than here. She considered how they could move his remains, but McCready was right. Gavin's ashes would collapse under their touch.

"He was good man," she said softly. Loch and McCready nodded in silent agreement. "We won't forget him."

There was so much more she could say, so much more that she *should* say, but the words would break the façade that was her composure. She touched his hand and the ash crumbled. That almost made her lose it, but Jayde gritted her teeth and snatched a handful of his ashes and stuffed them into the front pocket of her armor. She would bring him with her one way or another.

She stood up and headed back the way they'd come. The bodies of the lyscrens they had burned brought her some small joy. They might have taken Gavin from her crew, but her crew had taken many more of them. And if she had her way, they would kill many, many more of the aliens.

The trek up the tunnel to the entrance was much more difficult than the trek down. Jayde's legs burned with exertion and her lower back was beginning to ache from the strain of leaning forward. Although the air was cooler underground, the physical strain was making her sweat. The pain in her legs took her mind off Gavin, though. Once they got back to the ship and were in the free expanse of open space, the grief would hit her. It always did.

Jayde saw a beacon of light ahead and was relieved they were finally close to being back above ground. It had felt like they were down in the mine for days despite it really only being a few hours. They reached the entrance and Jayde stepped into the sunlight, thankful for the fresh air. She breathed in deep and looked around for Luther. His transport vehicle was still here, but she didn't see him.

"Luther?" she called out.

There was no reply. Loch and McCready stepped out of the mine and looked at her questioningly. She shrugged and walked over to the shed where he'd given them the flamethrowers. The door was ajar. Jayde grabbed onto the handle to pull it open fully and paused. There was blood splattered on the ground and part of the door. Her heart began pounding in her chest. Before she could pull the door open, McCready came up beside her and held his finger to his lips.

He gently pushed her hand off the handle and peered into the shed. A soft grunt escaped him and he pushed the door open forcefully. Jayde looked inside and saw Luther on the floor. He was lying face down with large claw marks down his back. Blood had pooled underneath his body.

"What happened to him?" Jayde said. "He looks like he was mauled by a bear."

"Those are lyscren claw marks," McCready corrected her. "They're not keeping to the mines, apparently. This might be the same one that got Gavin, considering they don't normally attack people."

Jayde felt sad for Luther. She'd only met him a few hours ago, but he seemed like a nice guy. Then she wondered how they were going to get paid when their employer was dead.

"Does he have any money on him?" Jayde asked. She immediately felt like scum, but what was a dead guy going to do with the money?

McCready searched Luther's pockets and produced a leather wallet full of plastic cards. "I'd say so," the soldier said. "Let's get back to town. Hopefully, Klaus has the engine fixed by now. I don't want to be here any longer."

"I'm driving," Loch said with an air of immaturity.

"You're the pilot," Jayde said. "You're supposed to drive."

Loch shrugged and climbed into the driver's seat and Jayde let McCready sit in the front with him. She wanted to be alone, but sitting by herself in the back of the vehicle would have to do. They started driving back to town and Jayde watched as the mine slowly faded into the distance. Her peace and quiet didn't last long.

"Uh, Jayde," Loch said.

"What is it?" she asked.

"We've got a problem."

Jayde turned to look out the front of the vehicle. Ahead, a small crowd of people was heading towards them. She counted at least twenty.

"What are they doing?" she asked.

"Probably coming to kill us," Loch answered. "Look at how they're walking."

Now that he'd pointed it out, Jayde realized the crowd of people weren't people.

They were sleepers.

7

MCCREADY LIFTED HIS SILVER Flux rifle and leaned out the side of the vehicle to take aim, then began blasting the sleepers to pieces. Loch turned the vehicle wide to try to pass around them, but the sleepers were too quick. The vehicle slammed into two of them with jarring force. Jayde was flung forward and almost bashed her head.

"Get us out of here!" she screamed.

Jayde unholstered her pistol and stood up, gripping the top of the vehicle with one hand and taking aim with the other. She fired off one shot and struck a sleeper in the neck. She growled in frustration. Her pistol only held a few rounds, and the jostling of the vehicle over the desert terrain wasn't helping.

The two sleepers they had hit were barely affected and tried to claw themselves around to the side windows. Jayde leaned left and managed a headshot to one of them. The sleeper's grip on the vehicle released and it went tumbling into the sand. She started to go for the second one, but McCready stuck the barrel of his rifle directly to the sleepers and head and pulled the trigger. Blood, brains, and bits of skull splattered in every direction.

Loch gunned the gas and the engine roared loudly in response. They fled past the remaining sleepers, leaving them behind in a cloud of dust. Jayde could see the outpost rising from the desert ahead. They weren't far now. She glanced back to see the sleepers were following them, but they couldn't keep pace with the cargo transport.

They made it another half mile before the engine made a grinding noise and died. The vehicle rolled to a stop. Loch tried to start the engine again, but nothing was happening. He looked back at Jayde and shrugged.

"I think the engine seized," he said.

"It looks like we're on foot the rest of the way," Jayde said. "Let's get moving before the sleepers catch up."

Jayde leaped down to the ground and started walking. McCready and Loch followed after her. The sand moved under her feet as she walked, making her ankle muscles burn with every step.

"If those people are sleepers or whatever, how do we know we're not walking into a town full of them?" Loch asked.

Jayde exchanged looks with McCready. She'd already had the same thought, but she had been smart enough to keep her mouth shut about it. Loch was terrible about not keeping his thoughts to himself.

"We'll figure that out when we get there," Jayde replied.

They walked in silence until they reached the outpost. The first thing Jayde noticed was the quiet.

Earlier, the town had been a bustling place of movement and noise. Now, it was eerily silent with no one in sight.

"Keep your eyes open," Jayde said. "I don't like this."

She led them toward the port where the *Determination* was waiting for them. They turned off the main street and Jayde saw her ship was still there, but it looked different. She stopped walking.

"What is it?" Loch asked.

"The *Determination*," she said. "The IDS is on."

The Immobile Defense System was a security feature she'd had installed that sealed the ship up tight, not allowing anyone in or out. It could only be activated from within the ship. She sighed in relief that Klaus appeared to be safe.

"I'm glad to see that Klaus didn't leave us behind," Loch said. "Or maybe the engine isn't fixed yet."

"Possibly," Jayde said.

She hoped that wasn't the case, but it was a possibility that Klaus hadn't finished the repairs, especially given the current situation. They began walking to the port platform, but a screech inside one of the buildings caught Jayde's attention. She jogged over to a window and glanced inside.

Overturned tables were angled together to create a makeshift wall and a woman was trapped behind them as a sleeper tried to reach her. She held a broken shaft of wood with a sharp end, but Jayde could tell the woman was too frightened to fight back.

"She needs our help," Jayde said. "I only see one sleeper in there."

"On it," McCready said.

He barged inside the building and laser fire filled the air. Jayde stepped inside as the sleeper's body crumpled to the floor.

"Oh God, thank you!" The woman shouted. She wiped the tears that were streaming down her cheeks. "I just couldn't bring myself to harm Jackson!"

"Forget that you ever knew him," Jayde said. "I know it sounds harsh, but trust me. The disease that took him made him into something different than anything you've known him to be."

Jayde glanced around the room. It appeared to be a bar. Tables and chairs were tipped over and broken glass littered the floor. "Where is everyone?" she asked.

"I'm not sure," the woman answered. "Everything was business as usual, and then suddenly there were screams and people began running. I thought I'd be safe in here, but then Jackson … that thing came in here. I heard shouts and blasts somewhere behind here, but it's been quiet for a while now. What happened? What's going on?"

"It's complicated, but you may be the only one left alive in this place. My ship is out there and we're leaving. If you want to come with us, you're welcome to." Jayde didn't normally like strangers on her vessel, but she couldn't leave the woman behind to die. The woman was speechless. Jayde gave her a moment to take in the information, then she motioned to the door.

"We've got to go. Now."

"I'll come with you," the woman said. "I've got to get something, then I'll be ready."

She pushed the tables aside and hurried across the room to the door, which was partially ajar. As soon as she opened it fully, a group of sleepers converged on the doorway and began clawing and biting her. Jayde cried out, but it was too late for the woman. McCready rushed over and kicked the woman clear of the doorway and slammed the door shut. Sleepers congregated at the windows, their hands slapping at the glass.

"This is insane," Loch said. He uprighted a chair and sat down, running his hands over his face and pushed his blonde hair off his forehead. "How did it spread so fast?"

Jayde wanted to know the same thing. Back on Ochillon, it had taken several hours for anyone to die, let alone become a sleeper. She looked out the window at the amassing crowd of sleepers. None of them looked dead. They all seemed to have turned like Gavin had, still alive and breathing when the disease took over.

Not getting an answer from anyone, Loch groaned. "We're going to die here, aren't we?"

"Not if I can help it," McCready said.

The old soldier disappeared into the back of the building and came back a few moments later. Jayde looked at him and he shook his head.

"No other way out," he said.

Jayde felt that she did her best under pressure, but this was more intense than anything they'd been through as a team before. She looked back to the window and saw the bloody face of the woman they'd rescued moments ago. Her face was twisted into an angry scowl and she scraped at the glass with her fingernails.

"Our only option is to get to the ship," Jayde said. "The question is, how? I've only got two shots left in my pistol and we left the flamethrowers in the cargo transport. What about your rifle?"

McCready checked the side of the weapon and grunted. "Fifty percent left. That'll get off a good number of shots, but I don't think it's going to be enough."

Jayde began pacing back and forth across the room, trying to figure out how they were going to escape. McCready went behind the bar counter and grabbed a bottle of something clear. He pulled the lid off and drank a deep gulp.

This is my crew, Jayde thought to herself. *I have to get us out of this mess. Great, McCready's resorted to alcohol. He's going to drink himself to death one day—*

"I got it," Jayde announced. "The alcohol."

"I'm all for getting drunk," Loch said, "but I don't think it's the best time for that."

"No, you idiot. We can light it on fire and use it to clear the sleepers out of the way so we can get to the ship. Are there rags back there?"

"Yeah," McCready answered. "Plenty of them, but only three bottles besides this one. The rest are broken."

Jayde went behind the bar with McCready and began pulling the lids off the bottles and cutting the rags into thin strips. She pushed the strips of cloth into the bottles and lit the ends of the cloth on fire.

"Don't use them all," McCready said. "We're out on the ship and I'd like to bring some back."

Jayde gave the soldier an unamused stare. McCready shrugged and downed the rest of the bottle he'd been drinking from, then hurled it against the wall. It shattered and sent glass flying.

"Let's do this or die trying," McCready grunted.

"Preferably the first one," Loch said.

Jayde handed a bottle to each of them and took one herself, then walked to the door. The noise of the sleepers made her skin crawl. It had been so long that she thought she would be lucky enough to never hear those sounds again. Fate had other ideas, apparently.

"You two ready?" Jayde asked.

"No, but who's ever ready for anything?" Loch answered.

"True. On the count of three, then." Jayde grabbed the door handle and made eye contact with Loch and McCready. "One, two, three."

She jerked the door open and let the two men hurl their bottles out first, then she risked a glance at the sleepers before tossing her bottle away from where the other two had thrown theirs. She banged the door shut and ran to the window. Flames were spreading from one sleeper to another, their proximity to each other helping the fire scatter among them.

"I think it's working," Jayde said.

The sleepers at the windows moved toward their fellows and Jayde grabbed a chair.

"Run like hell, boys!"

Jayde flung the chair into one of the windows, smashing the glass. She ran and leaped through the crude exit, catching the back of her hand on a shard of glass as she passed through. She landed in the dirt on her hands and knees and quickly stood up. The commotion had attracted the sleepers and they were coming toward her.

Loch came out of the window next, followed swiftly by McCready. The soldier began shooting into the crowd, taking down several of the sleepers. Jayde held off using her pistol in case they got into a bind.

"Let's go!" she screamed.

She ran towards the port and trusted that the other two were following. The port was as quiet as the outpost. No guards, no vendors, nothing. It was a strange sight compared to when they had first landed. The other thing she noticed was the *Determination* was the only ship docked. There were others when they landed. Jayde assumed they must have high-tailed it when the chaos happened.

"Almost there!"

Jayde's legs burned from the exertion, but she ignored the pain. They were almost to the dock platform. She could hear the sleepers following them, but she didn't dare turn around. It was as if she were reliving her past when she ran for the Convocation ship on Ochillon. Only this time she wasn't a scared little girl. She was a scared grown woman. Fear came in all ages.

She reached the platform and turned to see Loch and McCready not far behind. Her eyes widened as she saw what she guessed was a hundred sleepers coming their way.

"Don't stop!" she yelled. "Keep running!"

Loch stumbled but thankfully didn't fall. McCready grabbed the back of Loch's shirt and ran beside him, helping him the remainder of the distance. As soon as they stepped onto the platform, Jayde pulled up on the lever of the control panel that would raise the lift.

The lift didn't budge.

8

"IT'S NOT WORKING!" JAYDE cried out.

She pulled up and down on the lever forcefully, her heart pounding loudly in her chest as she watched the sleepers get closer and closer. She kicked the base of the panel in frustration and choked back the tears. McCready came to stand beside her and fired his rifle into the coming madness. He took down at least twenty, but for each one that went down, another took its place.

Jayde spun around and looked at the ship, trying to find some way to get up to the loading bay area. Although the IDS was on, if they could get to the doors then she would be able to get Klaus on the intercom and he could allow them inside.

"What do we do?" Loch asked her. Jayde could see the fear in his eyes. She was scared too, but she hoped that she hid her fear enough that he couldn't tell. She was the leader of their little band and leaders were supposed to be brave and fearless. Jayde felt like she was neither of those right now.

It was on the tip of her tongue to say she didn't know what to do. She was just about to open her mouth when an idea came to her. Jayde pointed up at the ship and forced a smile. She didn't know why, but she thought that would be inspiring.

"We're going to have to climb," she said. "Go!"

Loch gave her a look that said he thought she was insane, but he turned and started climbing up the side of the ship anyway. Jayde did the same thing. It wasn't an easy task, either. The metal was hot from sitting in the sun and there was very little to grab ahold of. Thin portions of steel offered small lips to clutch to with her fingertips, but as Jayde got higher up the side, she knew that one slip and she'd fall hard. Death was waiting nearby, eagerly anticipating her to die from the impact of a fall or from the bites of sleepers.

Jayde looked over her shoulder and saw McCready was still on the platform blasting sleepers with his rifle.

"McCready!" she shouted. "Get moving, now!"

She hoped he wasn't going to do anything stupid. If he didn't start climbing now, it would be too late for him. The army of sleepers was closing in on the platform.

"Throw me your gun!"

The soldier looked up at her and offered a glare. He didn't let anyone touch his rifle, but she didn't have time for his pride. She returned his scowl with her own and he finally relented. McCready fired off a few more blasts, then ran to the base of the ship and tossed his rifle up at her. Jayde held onto the ship with one hand and reached out to catch the weapon. She almost lost her hold and had to bite her lower lip to keep from screaming.

McCready began scaling the ship and Jayde fired off a few shots at the sleepers who got too close. Once the soldier was high enough above the ground, Jayde focused on climbing. It was difficult enough without carrying the rifle, but now her muscles were beginning to cry out in protest. *Almost there,* she told herself, forcing her arms and legs to obey her will.

Finally, blessedly, they reached the edge of the platform that led to the bay doors. Loch had already made it up and he helped her onto the platform. Jayde peered down at McCready and could tell he was struggling. It was difficult enough for herself, and the soldier's hands were much larger than hers.

"Keep an eye on him," Jayde told Loch. She handed him the rifle. "And don't tell him I let you hold this."

She stepped around Loch and pressed a button on the panel beside the doors. Her face scrunched as she saw blood on the button. She looked at her hands and realized the tips of her fingers were scraped and bleeding. A few of her nails were chipped as well, but she didn't feel any pain. Static buzzed through the speaker and Jayde waited impatiently for Klaus to answer. A long moment passed and still, there was nothing. She pressed the button again.

"Klaus," she spoke into the receiver at the bottom of the panel. "It's Jayde."

There was more static, but then Klaus's voice came back at her.

"Jayde? Thank God. I expected you back hours ago. I'm disabling the bay IDS now," he said.

Jayde backed up a step. There was a loud grinding noise and the steel panels covering the cargo bay doors slowly slid to the sides. The panels moved on a system of gears strong enough to push a thousand pounds and the panels disappeared into pockets that were hidden on either side of the doorway, offering up a deep *clang*.

The right-side bay door opened and Klaus stood there holding a rifle similar to McCready's. Klaus stepped out onto the platform and looked around.

"Where's McCready and Gavin?" he asked.

"McCready's coming. Gavin … didn't make it," Jayde said haltingly.

"What happened? I was working on the engine and I heard shouts. When I came up to see what the commotion was about, people were trying to get into the ship. At first, I thought they were the Convocation and that Loch had gotten into trouble or something."

"Thanks for the kind words," Loch muttered. "Take this back before McCready kills me." Loch handed the rifle back to Jayde.

"Once I realized they were just regular people, I engaged the IDS. They gave up trying to get in rather quickly after that."

"Probably because they were killed," Jayde said.

"What? What do you mean?"

"We encountered something down in the mineshaft. A lyscren bit Gavin on the hand. Within an hour or so he disappeared, and when we found him again, he'd turned into a sleeper."

"A sleeper? Wait. Are you sure it was a lyscren that bit him? Those things are harmless."

"I thought so, too," Jayde said. "This one was sick. Whatever it was carrying infected Gavin and he became a …" Jayde fumbled with how to explain what a sleeper was.

"A dredge," McCready said with a grunt as he climbed onto the platform to join them.

"Dredges are here?" Klaus asked in surprise. "How?"

"You know what a dredge is?" Jayde asked.

"I've never seen one in real life, but I've seen pictures and read documents about them. I thought they were only seen on Ochillon ten years ago and a handful of rural planets."

McCready walked past them and into the ship. Loch nodded to Klaus and followed after the soldier, leaving Jayde and Klaus alone.

"Gavin turned and tried to kill me and McCready. Loch saved us."

Klaus remained silent.

"When we got back to town, it became obvious that Gavin wasn't the only unlucky one. The entire place is full of sleepers. Or dredges, if you like McCready's term better."

"That's the Convocation's term," Klaus said.

"What do you mean? The Convocation knows about these things?"

"Absolutely. And I think they know more about them than they admit. They were there on Ochillon and dealt with the dredges, so they must know something. I wouldn't be surprised if they created the disease, whether intentional or accidental. They've tried to keep what happened on Ochillon a secret, but things always come to light."

That was a theory Jayde had never considered. Could the government really be behind the slaughter of her homeworld? If that were the case, then that meant the Convocation was responsible for her parents' deaths. Anger flooded her mind and she felt her face flush.

"Let's get off this cursed rock, shall we?" Jayde said.

"The repairs are done. I was just waiting for you guys to return."

"And if we didn't?"

Klaus smirked. "I'm no pilot, but I would have left all by myself if I had to."

They entered the ship and Klaus closed the bay door. He started to leave and Jayde re-engaged the IDS. Klaus looked at her questioningly.

"I'm not sure if those things can get up here or not, but I'm not taking any chances."

Klaus bowed his head and walked away. Jayde stood still for a moment, relieved to be back in familiar territory. The *Determination* was her home, and it was here within its metal walls that she felt the safest. She closed her eyes and took a deep breath, then headed for the observation deck.

Loch was already there sitting in his normal spot when she walked in. He'd changed out of his armor but still looked dirty. Jayde didn't blame him. As much as she wanted to wash the grime from her skin, she wanted to leave this place more. She took a seat in another chair and leaned back, placing her feet on the edge of a console.

"I still can't believe we left Gavin back there," she said softly.

"We did what we had to," Loch replied.

She knew that, but she still felt like she should have done more for him. He'd been with her long enough that he deserved better, whatever that looked like.

"How're the systems looking?" she asked, changing the subject.

"Everything looks good except the fuel level. It's higher than when we landed, but it's not at full capacity."

Fuel.

She'd forgotten all about the fuel with everything else going on.

"We need more fuel," she said. "We won't make it anywhere with less than a full tank, especially if we use the hyperdrive. Someone's got to go back out there."

"Send Klaus," Loch replied. "He missed all the fun earlier."

Despite the gravity of the situation, that did bring a smile to Jayde's face.

"That's not a bad idea. Keep it up and I just might stop hating you."

"How can you hate me? I'm the life of this crew."

Jayde rolled her eyes and stood up. "Seriously though, we need that fuel. I'm going back out there."

She left the observation deck before Loch could argue with her and stopped at her personal quarters to swap out the ammunition pack in her pistol. McCready's rifle was nice, but nothing beat her own weapon. Jayde holstered the gun on her waist and went back to the cargo bay. She didn't like the idea of scaling down the side of the ship, but there was no other choice.

Without a full tank of fuel, they might as well stay where they were and wait for the sleepers to kill them off. Jayde disabled the IDS and opened the same bay door Klaus had, then left the safety of the ship. She was preparing herself mentally for what she was about to do when she noticed the lift was level with the ship.

There was nobody on it, nor was there anyone on the platform with her. Had the blasted thing started working after they scaled up the ship? She supposed it was possible, but she had a feeling something wasn't right. Jayde drew her pistol and stepped over onto the lift. She looked down and saw the army of sleepers below. They were staring up at her, but they had no way of reaching her.

"That's weird," she whispered to herself.

Jayde followed the length of the ship with her eyes to where the fueling station was. It looked like the pump was still intact, but it was hard to tell for sure. She grabbed the lever and began lowering herself down the side of the ship, stopping when she was about the same height above the ground as the fueling pod, then she used another lever to move the lift horizontally. Once the lift was a few feet away from the pod, she released the lever and leaped across the gap to the other side.

She grabbed ahold of the nozzle handle and slid the nozzle into the ship's argon gas fuel tank and turned the pump on. Judging by the haphazard way the hose was laying, she assumed the port workers who had been fueling the ship had left in a hurry. Jayde glanced around every few seconds to make sure she was still alone, but she had the feeling someone was watching her. Once the tank was full, she turned the pump off and removed the nozzle, tossing it down carelessly.

And then Jayde knew why she felt eyes on her. Down on the ground was a little girl looking up at her. And the girl was surrounded by sleepers.

<h1 style="text-align:center">9</h1>

JAYDE'S INSTINCTS KICKED IN and she lowered the fueling station as fast as it would go.

The girl seemed oblivious to the danger. As soon as the lift touched the ground, Jayde leaped over the railing and ran towards the girl, drawing her pistol from its holster. The expression on the girl's face turned from confusion to fear.

"Get down!" Jayde shouted at her.

She didn't listen. Jayde was forced to shoot a sleeper who was perilously close to the girl and thankfully didn't miss the shot. The young girl seemed to have an epiphany and dropped to her hands and knees and began crawling across the dirt towards Jayde.

With the girl out of the way, Jayde started blasting at the sleepers furiously. Her nerves were shot and she couldn't get the image of Gavin's dead face out of her mind. Both of those things attributed to her missing as often as she hit her targets. The initial wave of the sleepers was down and Jayde knelt and grabbed the girl's hand, then pulled her up and dragged her to the fueling station lift.

Jayde forced the lift up and looked the girl over to make sure she hadn't been injured. Other than a few minor cuts and scrapes on her legs, the girl seemed fine. Jayde holstered her pistol.

"Where's your family?" Jayde asked.

"I don't know," the girl answered. "I was playing with my friends when one of those things came and tried to kill us. We got split up and I haven't been able to find anyone. You're the first person I've seen that isn't like them." The girl looked down at the sleepers.

"My name is Jayde. What's yours?"

"Sarah," the girl said.

"That's a nice name. My friends and I are leaving this planet, and you're going to come with us. You can't stay here. It's not safe."

Sarah nodded sadly. "Do you think my mom is dead?" she asked.

Jayde remembered being that young and watching everyone she knew die. It had made her into the strong woman she was today, and she didn't like telling lies.

"Yes, they are probably dead or have turned into one of the sleepers."

"Does it hurt? When someone becomes a sleeper?"

"I don't know," Jayde said.

Sarah didn't say anything else. The lift reached the fuel tank and Jayde angled the platform as close to the other lift as possible. There was a six-foot gap between them, and Jayde knew she could make the jump across, but she wasn't confident the girl could. The lift was as far over as she could get it though, so there was nothing else she could do.

"I'm going to jump to the other lift first, then you follow me."

"That seems pretty far," Sarah replied.

"You can do it. Watch me."

Jayde leaped across the gap and landed on the other lift. She turned to face Sarah and motioned for her to follow. Sarah hesitated, but she looked down at the sleepers below and seemed to make up her mind. She took a few steps back to get a running start and then jumped over the gap. Her feet barely landed on the edge of the lift and she started to fall back but Jayde grabbed onto her arm and pulled her to safety.

"I knew you could do it," Jayde said. She adjusted the lift back to its original spot and they rose up to the cargo bay. The bay door was cracked just as she'd left it. She ushered the girl onto the ship and through the door. McCready was standing there, rifle in his hands.

"What was that?" he said.

"What?"

"You went back out there *alone?* You could have been killed."

"I know," Jayde said. "I wasn't thinking clearly, but I'm fine. This is Sarah. She's coming with us."

McCready looked at the girl and offered his best attempt at a smile. Jayde hid her grin. He wasn't the smiling type. If anything, he looked more imposing with a smile than he did without one.

"Let's get going," Jayde said. "I don't want any more surprises. Or setbacks."

She led Sarah to the observation deck and offered her a seat near the window.

"Have you ever been off the planet?"

Sarah shook her head. "Never."

"You'll enjoy this, then. When we leave the atmosphere, you'll see fire around the ship. Don't worry, though. It's not going to hurt anything."

Jayde walked over to Loch and he nodded at Sarah. "Who's the girl?" he asked quietly.

"I found her outside. She was almost killed by sleepers."

"Contrary to what people say about you, I think you do have a heart," Loch joked.

"Who says I don't have one?" Jayde asked.

"Uh … I don't know," he answered. "But I'd punch anyone who said something like that."

"I doubt it," Jayde said with a chuckle. "Get us off this planet, pilot."

"My pleasure, Captain." Loch offered a mock salute and began pressing buttons on the console. The *Determination* shuddered as the ship's engines roared to life. The floor vibrated under Jayde's feet and the familiar hum of the ship settled over her. *Home,* she thought.

The ship began to rise from the dock and Jayde watched as the landscape of the planet began to fade from sight. She sat in the chair beside Sarah and the two of them stared out the window as they climbed further into the sky.

"All systems are reading steady," Loch said. "Everything's looking good. Charging the shields for the atmospheric exit."

As much as Jayde loved the open sea of space, there was something about the experience of entering and leaving an atmosphere that she loved. Maybe it was the symbolism. The knowledge that one could travel anywhere in the universe if you had the means. Yes, perhaps that was it.

"Prepare to leave M44," Loch said over the intercom system. "We're about to cross the threshold of the atmosphere."

A moment later, the glow of the ship's defenses filled the observation deck and the *Determination* was surrounded by a fiery wreath. The noise was loud and intense and Sarah covered her ears. It only lasted a few seconds since the ship was moving so quickly. They broke free of the planet's gravitational pull and entered the vastness of space.

"Wow," Sarah whispered. "It's beautiful."

"Yes, it is," Jayde agreed. She could still remember the first time she'd seen the beauty of space herself. "The universe is bigger than anything you can imagine. Trillions upon trillions of stars, millions of planets, and millions more alien lifeforms. You could travel through space your entire life and never see half of it."

"That's really big," Sarah said.

The two of them stared out the window in silence, enjoying the sight. Their peacefulness was quickly interrupted.

"We've got something incoming," Loch warned. "And it's coming fast."

"Can you tell what it is?" Jayde asked.

"It's a vessel, but I'm not sure what kind. It's *really* fast."

The space in front of the *Determination* began to form waves, much like an ocean or a lake, then the waves swirled into a vortex and a massive Convocation ship materialized out of hyperspace. It was a military vessel, and the ship's name was spelled out across the side in bold letters: BC NOMAD.

"It's a battlecruiser," Loch said. "What's a battlecruiser doing out here? Do you think they know about those sleeper things on M44?"

Jayde thought about what Klaus had said, about the Convocation knowing more about the sleepers and possibly even creating them. She thought of all the innocent people that had died down on M44, of Gavin … she clenched her jaw.

"We're getting a transmission," Loch said.

"Put it through," Jayde growled more forcefully than she intended.

Loch didn't say anything about her harshness. The screens above the window flickered to life and a uniformed man appeared.

"I'm Hans Otten, Captain of the *BC Nomad* and a general of the Convocation military. Identify yourself."

Jayde rose to her feet and stepped forward. "Captain Jayde Thrin of the *Determination.*"

Hans was an older man, older than McCready by at least ten years. His hair was gray and thin and his face was cleanly shaven. A plethora of medals and pins adorned the left lapel of his uniform and Jayde had a sinking feeling about general's arrival.

"How can we be of assistance?" Jayde asked.

"We received a distress call from M44. Have you been in contact with anyone on the planet?"

"I believe the distress is over," Jayde said. "We were on the planet. Everyone's dead except this girl." She motioned to Sarah.

"Dead? What happened?"

"Sleepers have overrun the entire place."

It was fleeting, but there was a slight twitch in Hans's eye. *He knows what they are,* Jayde thought. It added credence to Klaus's theory, and Jayde was starting to wonder just how much of that theory might be true.

"You know about them?" she asked.

"I do," Hans answered. "I did *not* know that the situation on M44 was that dire."

"I don't think anyone did. The people weren't prepared for what happened."

"Is anyone on board your vessel injured or sick? The disease spreads quickly upon contact with an infected subject."

"No. We lost a man down there, but no one on board is infected."

"Good. You won't mind if we board you and check just to be sure, then?"

Jayde knew when to pick her battles. She didn't like strangers on her ship, and especially not someone from the Convocation, but if it aided in getting far away from M44, then so be it.

"Not at all," she said. "We'll prepare to be boarded."

"Thank you, Jayde. Just one thing. Make sure nobody is armed, will you? My men have seen a lot of … surprises lately and they can be a little on edge."

"Not a problem," Jayde replied.

"I'll see you shortly."

The picture on the screen faded and Jayde took a deep breath. There were only a handful of people on her ship, so she assumed this check would be quick and painless. She turned to Loch.

"Get us ready," she said. "I need to find McCready."

Jayde left the observation deck and headed to the old soldier's quarters. She found McCready lying in bed, staring up at the ceiling.

"We're about to be boarded by a Convocation ship," Jayde said. "Keep your rifle out of reach, if you don't mind."

"Will do," McCready said. "What are they boarding us for? Did they finally track Loch down?"

Jayde laughed. "No. They received a distress signal from M44 and want to ensure none of us are infected."

"Do you mind needles?"

"No, why?"

"They're going to check everyone's blood. That's how they'll know if someone is infected."

"Can I ask you something?" Jayde said.

"Of course," McCready replied.

"Is the Convocation responsible for the sleepers?"

McCready turned his attention to her. He was silent for a long moment before saying, "I don't think so. Everything I experienced told me they were confused about its origins. Does that mean they aren't hiding something? Of course not. The government always provides the biggest smokescreens."

The soldier turned his eyes back to the ceiling. "Who's the captain of the ship?" he asked.

"Hans Otten."

"He's a good man," McCready said. "I didn't serve under him, but I heard nothing but decent things about him."

"That's good to know. I just wanted to let you know they were coming before they came in here and surprised you."

"Thanks."

Jayde headed for the eastern side of the ship where the two vessels would connect. She reached the steel door to find the *Determination* was already linked to the *BC Nomad*. That had to be the smoothest docking she'd ever experienced. The ships hadn't banged together at all.

"Pressurizing the docking hall," Loch's voice came over the intercom. "Three, two, one. Manual override enabled on the doors. We're all set."

Jayde unsealed the door and looked through the porthole. Her eyes widened in surprise as a group of Convocation soldiers kicked the door open, which slammed into her and sent her reeling backward.

"Hands up!" one of them shouted.

Her vision was spinning, but Jayde did as she was ordered. She could feel something warm sliding down her cheek and assumed it was blood. More soldiers entered her ship and swarmed down the hallways. The last person to enter was Hans. He stepped into the ship and looked down at her, distrust clearly plastered across his face.

<h1 style="text-align:center">10</h1>

"Captain Jayde Thrin. From Ochillon."

His words sounded like an accusation. Jayde rubbed the side of her head and glared at the man.

"Yeah?"

"The sole survivor of a planet-wide calamity. Tell me, Jayde, how did you survive?"

"Technically I wasn't the only one to get off the planet," Jayde said. "There were ten of us, but one was infected and killed everyone else. I was lucky to live."

Hans looked at one of his soldiers. "Check her."

The soldier handed his rifle to another man and retrieved a small black box from his pack, then knelt beside Jayde and opened the box. There was a device with a needle attached and he jabbed the needle into her arm. He wasn't gentle about it, either.

Jayde grimaced but didn't make a noise. The screen on the machine counted backward from ten and then beeped loudly. A green light flashed and the soldier removed the needle.

"She's clean," he said.

"Help her up," Hans ordered.

The soldier offered his hand to Jayde, but she slapped it away and stood up on her own.

"My apologies for the roughness," Hans said. He clasped his hands behind his back. "One can never be too cautious these days."

"Right." Jayde didn't bother to hide her anger.

"How many people are on your crew?"

"Four. We picked up the girl I told you about on the planet. She was the only survivor we encountered that didn't get killed."

"This shouldn't take long, then."

"What's a battlecruiser doing this far from the established colonies?" Jayde asked.

Hans regarded her quietly for a moment. "I told you, we received a distress signal."

"And you happened to be in the area?"

The general smiled. Jayde guessed he must be picking up on her assumption.

"I don't know what you might be implying, but yes, we happened to be in the area. Contrary to whatever you might believe, we've been patrolling this end of the universe for several months now. There's been an increased number of Thraan sightings and we're making sure they aren't doing anything depraved."

Jayde knew plenty about the Thraan. Anyone who flew on a ship knew about them, but Jayde had never encountered the alien species. They were barbaric creatures, attacking and killing any human settlements they came across. She assumed the Thraan were out here on the fringe of civilization because it would be less likely they would encounter resistance.

"Have you seen any?"

"None," Hans said. "That doesn't mean they aren't hiding out here, though. They're clever creatures, I'll give them that."

The soldiers who had swarmed her ship slowly started returning. The last group came back with Sarah. Jayde frowned.

"What are you doing with her?" she asked.

The soldiers ignored her and brought Sarah to Hans.

"They're all clean, except this one. She's not infected, but her blood has an anomaly I've never seen before."

"Let me see."

Hans held the device with the needle up and stared at the screen. His face scrunched and he seemed troubled. He handed the device back to the soldier and looked at Jayde.

"Your crew is clean, so you're all set. I'm taking the girl with me. Our scientists will want to take a closer look at her."

"What for?"

"That's nothing for you to concern yourself with," Hans replied. "Get back to the ship," he ordered his men. The soldiers started filing into the docking hall. Jayde watched them in silence, wondering what they planned on doing with Sarah. The girl looked pleadingly at her, but Jayde knew there was nothing she could do to stop them.

Besides that, she didn't know what to do with a child on her ship. Jayde ran a crew of mercenaries and they had made a lot of enemies over the years. The last thing she wanted was the blood of a child on her hands.

Jayde avoided Sarah's gaze and stared at Hans instead. The remaining soldiers ushered Sarah across the docking hall and into the *BC Nomad*.

"You might want to bomb M44," Jayde said.

"I planned on it," Hans replied. "We don't need that disease spreading to any other planets. Thank you for your cooperation, Jayde. I appreciate it."

Jayde shrugged and watched the general leave her ship. She shut the door and stared through the porthole. She could see Sarah struggling against the soldiers, trying to break free of their grasp. Jayde sighed. She felt bad for the girl.

Once the docking hall was clear, Jayde pressed a button on the intercom beside the door.

"Go ahead," Loch said.

"De-pressurize the hall. It's clear."

"I will as soon as the door closes on their side."

Jayde thought the door was closed, but when she looked through the porthole again, she saw that was not the case. The door was ajar, but she didn't see anyone. *Maybe they forgot to close the door,* she thought.

And then she saw the blood. It sprayed onto the door like torrential rain. Jayde cried out, thinking that Hans had Sarah killed. A body fell into the doorway, but it wasn't Sarah's. It was one of the soldiers. Jayde unsealed the door and sprinted across the hall. She slowed her pace as she got closer. The sound of laser fire echoed into the chamber and screams assailed her ears. She reached for her pistol but it wasn't there. She forgot that she left it in her personal quarters.

The face of the soldier on the ground stared off blankly in death, his mouth open at an odd angle. His rifle was in his hands, his finger on the trigger. Jayde retrieved the gun and pushed the door to the *BC Nomad* open further and cautiously peered inside. There were more bodies and a lot more blood.

Jayde stepped into the ship and held the rifle up, ready to shoot the first thing that moved. One of the bodies reached for her and she jumped backward. The rifle was equipped with a flashlight and she flipped the switch on and pointed the beam of light at the body.

It was Hans.

"Oh, God. What happened?" Jayde asked.

"The girl," Hans rasped. Blood dripped down his lower lip. "She's not … human." He coughed and showered the floor with more blood. "Go. Warn the others."

"The others? Who? Warn who?" Jayde didn't know what he was talking about.

"The Convoca—" Hans coughed again and Jayde could tell by the sound that blood was filling his throat. "Warn them about the Thraan."

A clattering sound in the shadows captured Jayde's attention. She started backing away from Hans. Glittering eyes appeared in the darkness and Jayde's heart started hammering in her chest. She lifted the rifle and fired off a shot. The eyes disappeared and there was more noisy movement.

It was coming for her. She scrambled into the docking hall and tried to move the soldier's body out of the doorway, but he was heavier than he looked. Jayde's hands began shaking uncontrollably and she screamed when she heard something nearing the door. She gritted her teeth and fired the rifle at the dead man's leg, blasting it from the rest of his body. She grabbed the door and pulled it shut.

Jayde sprinted to the *Determination*. Something was scraping at the door behind her, but she dared not look. She stumbled as she reached her ship and fell face-first onto the floor. She rolled onto her back and kicked the door shut, then struggled to her feet and sealed the door.

"De-pressurize the hall!" Jayde screamed into the intercom.

"I told you, I can't until they close their door!"

Jayde's heart fell into her stomach. She looked into the porthole and saw the door was open again. Something large and scaly was coming.

"Break away now! Now, Loch!"

The *Determination* shuddered and rocked roughly as it pulled away from the *BC Nomad*. The docking hall fractured and broke into pieces. The creature that had been Sarah floated away slowly into space. Jayde continued to watch until she couldn't see the creature anymore. The *BC Nomad* was tilting awkwardly and gradually began to draw closer to M44.

The ship entered the atmosphere of the planet and Jayde turned from the window to see Loch standing there watching her.

"What …" words failed him.

"I don't know," Jayde said. "I'm so confused. I don't know." She slid down the door and sat on the flooring, letting the gun fall from her grasp. "That could have been me," she whispered softly. "On Ochillon, that could have been my fate. Turning into one of those … those things."

Loch knelt in front of her and looked into her eyes.

"But it didn't happen to you," he said. "You're still here. You're alive."

Tears streamed down Jayde's cheeks and she started sobbing. Loch sat next to her and wrapped his arms around her, hugging her close. She buried her face into his neck and cried for a long time. Loch didn't say anything. He just held her and let her shed the tears she'd been holding in.

The tears for Gavin. For her parents. For Sarah. And for herself. It was selfish, she knew, but she didn't care. She was always the strong one, always the one who had to lead and make decisions. She knew what needed to be done, but she didn't want to do it. She didn't want that responsibility.

Eventually, Jayde calmed down and wiped the salty tears from her face. Hans's words echoed in her mind over and over. *She's not human. Warn the others.* How had a Thraan taken a human form? Or had it? Maybe the girl had been infected like Gavin, but her body had a different reaction to the infection? It was too much. Things weren't adding up, but she had a growing suspicion that what had happened on Ochillon wasn't a fluke.

It had to be part of something bigger. It had to have been planned by someone or something. She'd had her doubts about the Convocation being involved, but now she was sure that they had nothing to do with the sleepers. They were trying to figure out what was happening just as Jayde was.

Nothing was going to change if she just sat in her ship and cried. Jayde rose to her feet and Loch stood as well. She looked out the porthole one more time.

M44 was in the distance now, too far to see anything other than a sphere the color of dirt.

Jayde considered again what needed to be done. She didn't want the responsibility, but if she didn't warn the Convocation, who would? McCready was with her no matter what, and Klaus didn't care where they went or what they did so long as he got paid. Loch, however, was a different matter. His warrants would almost certainly deter him, and she couldn't force him to do anything. He was a paid member of her crew, not a slave.

"I know what has to be done, but you're not going to like it."

Loch raised an eyebrow at her in curiosity.

"It's going to be a long journey, and it might not be safe for you. I want to be honest with you about that. And I also want to be honest with you and say that I need you, Loch. I *need* you for this. I know I bust your balls about your women and everything, but it's nothing personal. You know that, right?"

Loch nodded slowly, seeming confused. "Yeah, I know that. What's going on, Jayde? Just spit it out already, will you?"

Jayde smiled at him. He'd grown on her. At first, she couldn't stand him. He was a good pilot, and that's why she had hired him, but he was so much more than just hired help. Loch was her friend, and that's why she wanted him on board for this mission. She stood up tall.

"Set a course for Earth."

ABOUT THE AUTHOR

Richard Fierce is a fantasy and space opera author. He's been writing since childhood, but began publishing in 2007. Since then, he's written multiple novels and short stories.

In 2000, Richard won Poet of the Year for his poem *The Darkness*. He's also one of the creative brains behind the Allatoona Book Festival, a literary event in Acworth, Georgia.

A recovering retail worker, he now works in the tech industry when he's not busy writing.

He's married and has three step-daughters (pray for him), three dogs (huskies!), a cat, and two ferrets. He basically has a zoo.

His love affair with fantasy was born in high school when a friend's mother gave him a copy of *Dragons of Spring Dawning* by Margaret Weis and Tracy Hickman.